Dear Parent:

Congratulations! Your child is taking the first steps on an exciting journey. The destination? Independent reading!

STEP INTO READING® will help your child get there. The program offers five steps to reading success. Each step includes fun stories and colorful art. There are also Step into Reading Sticker Books, Step into Reading Math Readers, Step into Reading Phonics Readers, Step into Reading Write-In Readers, and Step into Reading Phonics Boxed Sets—a complete literacy program with something for every child.

Learning to Read, Step by Step!

Ready to Read   Preschool–Kindergarten
• big type and easy words • rhyme and rhythm • picture clues
For children who know the alphabet and are eager to begin reading.

Reading with Help   Preschool–Grade 1
• basic vocabulary • short sentences • simple stories
For children who recognize familiar words and sound out new words with help.

Reading on Your Own   Grades 1–3
• engaging characters • easy-to-follow plots • popular topics
For children who are ready to read on their own.

Reading Paragraphs   Grades 2–3
• challenging vocabulary • short paragraphs • exciting stories
For newly independent readers who read simple sentences with confidence.

Ready for Chapters   Grades 2–4
• chapters • longer paragraphs • full-color art
For children who want to take the plunge into chapter books but still like colorful pictures.

STEP INTO READING® is designed to give every child a successful reading experience. The grade levels are only guides. Children can progress through the steps at their own speed, developing confidence in their reading, no matter what their grade.

Remember, a lifetime love of reading starts with a single step!

Step into Reading, Random House, and the Random House colophon are registered trademarks of Random House, Inc.

Visit us on the Web!
StepIntoReading.com
randomhouse.com/kids

Educators and librarians, for a variety of teaching tools, visit us at RHTeachersLibrarians.com

ISBN: 978-0-449-81388-1 (trade) — ISBN: 978-0-375-97156-3 (lib. bdg.)
Printed in the United States of America
10 9 8

nickelodeon™

BUBBLE GUPPIES™

THE BEST DOGHOUSE EVER!

By Mary Tillworth

Cover illustrated by Sue DiCicco and Steve Talkowski

Interior illustrated by MJ Illustrations

Based on the screenplay
"Build Me a Building!" by Adam Peltzman

Based on the TV series *Bubble Guppies,*
created by Robert Scull and Jonny Belt

Random House 🏠 New York

We love Bubble Puppy!

He is a great pet.

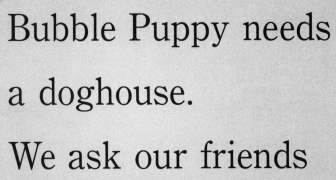

Bubble Puppy needs
a doghouse.
We ask our friends
for help.

The crabs draw a plan.

It is a doghouse.

9

We get wood and nails.

We get paint and tools,
too.

We put on

our hard hats.

The hats

keep us safe.

It is time to start.

We check

the house plan.

14

Zip, zip, zip!

A crab saws wood.

16

Bang, bang, bang!
We hammer the nails.

Twist, twist, twist!
A crab turns
the screw.

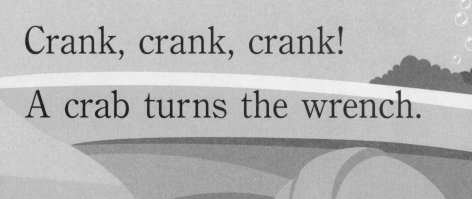

Crank, crank, crank!

A crab turns the wrench.

The house is done!

We show Bubble Puppy.

Bubble Puppy
toots the horn.

He loves
his new doghouse.

All right!
We built
the best doghouse ever!